HIS BEST
SCORE

SISTERS LOOKING FOR A FEW GOOD MEN BOOK 5

OLIVIA HOUDE

—

His Best Score

Olivia Houde © 2022

TABLE OF CONTENTS

HIS BEST SCORE
Olivia Houde

Felicia Grace is a Graphic Designer and part-time educator at the local Community Center. She loves inspiring and captivating others through her visual designs. Working with underprivileged children is her way of giving back.

Ronald Taylor, a professional Football player, and star running back for the Baltimore Ravens, is at the top of his game and looking forward to winning the upcoming Superbowl game against the Washington Commanders.

They clash when he comes to speak with youths at the Community Center. The attraction is instant. Let the games begin. Can he let go of the pain in his past? Will she accept the promise of a brighter future?

1

FELICIA

I COCK MY HEAD TO THE SIDE, taking a long look at the screen. I'm happy with the design I've come up with. The client is an entrepreneur with an up-and-coming whole foods cereal brand, and they hired me to do an eye-catching design. Something modern and fresh, they said. I let out a satisfied sigh. I'm pretty sure I nailed it.

I run my hands through my curly hair, a surge of anxiousness filling me as I attach the document to the email and hit send. Finally, it's finished, the project I spent the last week working on. I hope the client is every bit as thrilled with the results as I am.

I close down my laptop and head to the community center for my afternoon shift. I volunteer there every Saturday, and sometimes Sundays too. Working with underprivileged children comes with its own struggles, but for the most part, I love my work there. It feels so good to be giving back to my community, especially since I was once one of those kids.

I walk through the front doors expecting it to be like any other Saturday. My job as an educator is to teach youth about the programs and assistance available to them, no matter what they're going through. Most days, I just sit in a classroom-like setting with the kids around a semicircle of desks.

But today is different.

"Felicia Grace, the exact woman I wanted to see!" Darcie, our lead coordinator, is beaming as I walk into the main foyer.

"Good afternoon, Darcie! What's up?"

"I've been waiting for you to get here, actually," she explains. "We have a very special guest speaker here today, and he asked if we had anyone that could assist him for the afternoon. So, I thought who better than you, right? You're my top gal, and you know as much about this place and how it runs as I do. Plus, I think you'll be excited when you find out who it is."

I follow her as she continues talking, heading into the main assembly room. It's a weathered room with a makeshift stage and folding chairs that have seen better days where our guest speakers give their presentations.

I feel my stomach clench into knots when I see him: Ronald Taylor.

He's the hunky half-black, half-Samoan star running back for the Baltimore Ravens. I've never been much of a football fan, but even people who aren't into sports know who he is. He's a legend around here, the best running back we've had in over a decade. His legacy has extended from playing football to doing sports drink commercials and starting his own non-profit.

And giving speeches at community centers, apparently.

He smiles at me when I walk into the room and, though I don't want it to, it causes an aching between my thighs. I'm sure he's a typical jock, cocky and overzealous, but I'd have to be blind in both eyes to deny how handsome he is.

"Hey," he says, extending a hand to me once I'm beside him. "Ron."

I smile sweetly and place my hand in his, enjoying the warmth of his skin on mine. "Pleased to meet you. I'm Felicia, Felicia Grace."

"Felicia? Pretty," he says with a smirk, and I immediately assume he says that to all the women he meets. My name could be Helga or Sausageflaps, and he would have said the same thing, I'm sure.

"You work here?"

"Sort of. I'm an educator here. I work with youth to teach them about our programs and the different resources available to them. I'm actually a volunteer, though."

"Hmm, pretty *and* sweet as hell. I like that."

The way my heart's fluttering is infuriating. I don't want to be affected by this Greek God of a human, yet my body insists on betraying me. My knees have a slight wobble every time he smiles at me, and I can't think straight when our eyes are locked.

"What's your speech about today?"

"I'm here to talk to the kids about how you can achieve your dreams if you put your mind to it and put in the work. Nothing is out of reach if you commit one-hundred ten percent, you know?"

It takes everything in me to keep from rolling my eyes. *Great, another bigwig athlete just here to spoon-feed the kids dribble about how life is nothing but a fairy tale. You can be anything you want kids if you just believe. An NFL star, an astronaut, a dinosaur. What a crock.*

"Well, I don't think *anything* is possible," I say, averting my gaze. "Even with hard work, some stuff just isn't attainable for everyone."

Damn, why am I one of those people? The kind that judged a person without knowing them. Taking their measure on my own preconceived bias. He probably thinks I'm a nut.

"Wow, you are one of those. I should have known. Normally I could spot one of you a mile away." Ron says to me. "But you're hidden in a pretty package with a smile so genuine, so beguiling, and so seductive, I just wanted to fall in and take a swim."

"What is that supposed to mean? I have no idea what you are trying to say." Felicia fires back.

"One thing I do believe to be the truth is that if you truly want something and it is within your power to make it happen, then only you can stop your dream from happening, forget the naysayers in your life or the people that try to bring you down. I'm not someone that got where I am from dreaming it into a reality." Ronald replies

She has no idea who I am.

2

———

RONALD

THE WAY SHE LOOKS AWAY makes me want to grab her and kiss her. She didn't initially strike me as a negative person, but there's a sadness to her voice that tells me she's been let down by people before. Probably by life.

"Maybe you'd think anything was possible if you spent some time around me. I have a way of making miracles happen."

"Is that so?" she snaps, cocking her head to the side as she folds her arms over her chest. "Nothing like being a self-declared miracle worker."

"It's not a self-declaration," I correct. "Countless people have told me that great things, incredible things, tend to happen when I'm around. Why my own Mama said so last week when I was at her house."

"Oh yeah? Why, what happened?"

"Her kitchen faucet broke while I was there, and I managed to fix it for her. Not to toot my own horn, but I'm more than good looks and innate athletic ability. I'm also pretty handy."

Felicia laughs so hard she snorts, shaking her head at me. "So, the amazing thing was that your Mama's dishwasher *broke* while you were there? Things breaking around you, that's amazing and should entice me to be around you more?"

I can't help but laugh when I realize how ridiculous it sounds. "The lucky part wasn't that it broke; the lucky part was that it broke *while I was there.* So, I could fix it. If I wasn't around, she would'a had to call a plumber and spend a fortune getting it fixed."

"All the money you make, and you make your mama pay for her own home repairs?"

I feel a rush of crimson heat overtake my face. "No! Of course, I would have paid for it … if she had let me. My mama's stubborn."

"Well, that's one thing we have in common then." Felicia smiles at me, the first genuine smile I've seen on her since she walked into this room.

"Even though I'm well off now, she still seems to think we're poor. She won't come to me when she has troubles. I always have to pry the news out of her when she needs anything."

"Can't blame her for wanting to make it on her own. Nothing wrong with a strong, independent woman doing her own thing. Men always feel like they have to swoop in and save a lady just because she's single as if that instantly qualifies her as some damsel in distress. Some people just like being able to make a go of it on their own, stand on their own two feet."

"I respect that," I say. "I just wish my mama would let me help her more … because I love her, and she did so much for me growing up. She worked three jobs to keep a roof over our heads and food in our bellies. She paid for school supplies and field trips, even when the soles of her shoes were worn through. I just wanna pay her back, even a little, for all she sacrificed."

Felicia's demeanor softens, her arms unfolding as she stares up at me with those big, dark eyes. Like two black holes floating amongst the galaxy, I wonder how many stars have been lost to them.

"Maybe you're a better man than I originally took you for, Ron Taylor."

Ron folded his arms across his chest so he wouldn't yank Felicia into his arms and kiss her senseless. She looked so damn delicious in that long, black striped dress. From the way the fabric cupped her high, firm breasts, he wondered if she was even wearing a bra. He didn't like the thought of her being braless and other men watching her.

Why is that?

When it came to something he wanted

3

WE STAND THERE TOGETHER, staring into one another's eyes for what feels like an eternity. It isn't until Darcie comes back into the room chattering away excitedly that Ron and I remember where we are and why he's here.

His presentation goes off without a hitch. Although I have to admit, his speech about achieving your dreams is a lot less phony and way more awe-inspiring than I had anticipated. He tells the kids about his childhood, how his dad left when he was barely two and how hard his Mama worked to make ends meet. The whole thing is very touching, and I even find myself tearing up at certain parts.

When it's over, and the kids have all left, he flags me over from across the room. He's cleaning up juice boxes and paper plates with half-eaten snacks still on them, and something about seeing him look so human and ordinary is endearing.

"What's up?" I ask. "Need help tidying up?"

"No, that's okay. I mean unless you want to. I was actually going to ask what you're doing after this."

My heart slams against my ribcage, choking me up and making it impossible to form a coherent sentence. "I … Sorry, what?"

"What are you doing after this? I mean, now. Do you have plans?"

"No, I … No plans."

"Cool. Would you wanna go out to get something to eat? There's this great seafood shack a couple of blocks from here. Do you like seafood?"

"Love it. It's one of my favorites. Do you seriously want to get a bite to eat? With me? Right now?"

Ron laughs. "Yeah. Why are you saying that like it's so hard to believe?"

"No, no reason. I'm just … I'm surprised, that's all."

"Yeah? And why's that?"

"Don't you get hit on by like … model cheerleaders and stuff all day? Don't you have a girlfriend? There's no way a guy as successful and handso … well off … as you are single."

He grins, no doubt catching my nearly calling him *handsome.* "Well, I know it comes as a surprise, but I'm a thousand percent single right now. I haven't had a girlfriend in over a year, actually. The last one was … Let's just say it ended on a very bitter note and kinda scared me off women for a while."

My brain feels guarded, as though I shouldn't believe these lines and these stories so easily, but my heart detects a sincerity to his voice. I want to believe he's telling the truth, that this isn't some ruse to get me in bed and then never call me again.

"Alright, fine," I say, "but you're buying, and it's *just* dinner, no hanky panky. So don't get any wild ideas."

"That's fine. Some dinner company is all I'm looking for."

Sure, sure. Bet you say that to all the ladies too.

We finish cleaning up the community center and head out, enjoying the unusually warm winter weather as we walk. Trees line the streets, their branches all covered in blankets of white snow. It makes for a beautiful view, and if I weren't so determined to keep this date friendly, I'd say it was borderline romantic.

"After you," he says, holding open the door to Joe's Crab Shack. I step inside, the smells of fried fish and tartar sauce tickling my nose. It's been a long time since I had some good fish and chips, and my stomach rumbles loudly as we sit down.

"So, tell me a little bit about you," he says while we wait for the waitress to make her way over to us.

"Me? What do you want to know? There isn't much to tell, really to sum it up. My mama had three sisters, got married young, and had six daughters, and you talked to my sister Sharon on the phone regarding your ring. She owns a few lingerie boutiques, and I have several cousins spread out all over the country. So, a very large and nosey family is what I've got. I work as a graphic designer, and when I'm not doing that, I'm volunteering at the community center. I put myself through design school by working at a record store and selling shoes. I've led a pretty ordinary life, really."

"You work from home?"

The question takes me off guard. "Yeah. Why?"

He shrugs. "No reason. I always thought it'd be quite nice. You know, to be that grounded. Not have to get dressed if you don't want to. Nowhere to drive to, no planes to catch. It just sounds so … peaceful."

To say I'm shocked would be an understatement, but I don't say it. From the outside looking in, Ron's life seems to be perfect. He makes millions of dollars playing professional football, a career most only dream of. He gets to travel the world and do what he loves. It shocks me that he would envy my life in any way.

"You don't like traveling?"

"No, I do. It's just a lot. Even the house I bought myself, I mean, yeah, it's six-thousand square feet, but I'm not even there to appreciate it a lot of the time. Sometimes having a quieter life would be nice, you know?"

I raise an eyebrow at him. "No, I don't. All I hear is a grown-ass man sitting there complaining about how successful he is, and how he's not home to enjoy his mansion enough. Sounds like a lot of bullshit if you ask me."

He sighs as he stares out the window. "Never mind. Figured you wouldn't get it." His voice is so soft and so sad, and I suddenly feel like the biggest a-hole in the universe.

4

———

RONALD

MAYBE THIS DATE wasn't such a good idea after all. Not that it's technically a date, at least not as anything more than acquaintances. My heart feels deflated as I realize she doesn't get it, doesn't get me. Just like everyone else.

"I'm sorry," she says, placing her hand on top of mine. I wish she'd leave it there forever. Her buttery soft skin melts the sadness residing in me, and everything starts to shift when I look into her eyes and see the warmness radiating from her.

"It's okay; I shouldn't have said that" I say. "I shouldn't be sitting here complaining about all I have, especially to someone who … Not that I think your life isn't great, but__"

"No, it's okay. I get it. I don't have what you have; you don't have to sugarcoat it. It's just fact, plain and simple. I shouldn't have bitten your head off for trying to tell me what about my life you think is worth appreciating. But you're right; there's something nice about the quietness and feeling grounded. There's a peacefulness to knowing I can roll out of bed and start my day."

I smile at her, though my heart aches when she pulls her hand away. *Maybe she does get it.*

"Are you guys ready to order?"

The waitress is cute, her bubbly voice and personality providing an upbeat air to Joe's Crab Shack, but she's got nothing on Felicia Grace.

"Do you want to take our food to go?" Felicia asks. "We could eat it back at my place if you want."

I feel my cock twitch in my pants at the thought, then silently scold myself. She's not hitting on me; she's just trying to be friendly. I can't let my body run away with fantasies of more than what this really is.

"I'd like that," I tell her.

5

———

FELICIA

I TOSS THE BAG OF FOOD onto the coffee table as I grab Ron and press my lips against his. He's surprised, I can feel it, but he kisses me back as our mouths meld together in sweet harmony. I don't know what I'm doing, but it feels too damn good to stop.

"Hey, are you … are you sure you want this?"

He's more of a gentleman than I took him for. Sure, he's buff and successful and a bit conceited, but he's also dreamy, hardworking, and selfless, and those are all qualities that make him worth being with.

"I'm sure," I say, pulling him into another kiss. His hands reach around and cup my cheeks, squeezing as he lifts me up. I wrap my legs around him as we continue to kiss, thinking about how this could only be hotter if we were both naked and he had me pinned up against a wall.

He sets me down just long enough to flip my shirt off over my head. My hands scramble to get my jeans undone and pulled down, and I nearly trip as I fight to get my feet out of the pant legs. Ron laughs softly but doesn't say anything; he just tore off his jacket and threw his shirt somewhere on my floor.

I wrestle out of my bra and panties, leaving me completely naked. He quickly follows suit, sliding his jeans and boxers off and kicking them somewhere behind him. His skin, light against mine, is delicious and smooth as he rests both my thighs on his hips again.

At first, I think I'm going to get my wish and that he's going to take me there right up against the wall, but instead he carries me into the kitchen and flicks on the light. I don't have time to ask what he's doing before he sets me on the counter and puts his mouth on me, hot and wet, his tongue teasing my opening before making its way up to my clit.

I grab his head to pull him closer as my ass and hips start to buck faster and faster against his face. I feel the pressure building and wet juices sliding down my inner thighs. He then presses a finger inside me, burying that thick digit deep inside me and making a *cum hither* motion.

"Ron, I … I think I'm gonna. __"

"Cum for me," he says, breaking contact with me just long enough to get the words out.

I scream out in ecstasy as an orgasm overtakes me like a tidal wave, pulling me deep and sucking me under in a sea of pleasure. My mind goes blank as I fight to process how good it feels, and it takes a few moments to realize that I've been flipped over and am now bent over my kitchen counter, my dripping pussy still quivering in the aftermath of my climax.

Everything I have is presented to him, bare and raw, and all I want is for him to take me now and claim me as his own.

6

RONALD

HER GORGEOUS LITTLE SLIT is just there for the taking, waiting for me to enter. I grab my manhood, thick and dripping with precum, and line it up with her opening. My head parts her lips as I make my way inside, and I see her hands grip the counter as I fill her inch by inch.

I feel myself stretching her, her tight cavern opening bit by bit to welcome me inside. It isn't until I've fit the last inch of me inside her that I lean forward and kiss her back and shoulder blade.

"Mmm, you feel so good," she whimpers.

"So do you," I tell her. I grab her hips as she tightens her grasp on the counter, sliding myself almost all the way out of her before thrusting back inside. She lets out a small cry every time my gems slap the back of her legs, her pussy quivering around my thick tool.

"Don't stop, don't stop," she chants, the words making my balls clench.

I don't want to cum yet, but I don't know how much longer I'll be able to hold off in this position. So, I stop and pull her arms behind her back, standing her up and placing my mouth right beside her ear.

"Let's move to the couch," I say, to which her only response is an enthusiastic nod.

I keep her hands clasped behind her back as I lead her to the couch, only turning her around once she's standing beside it. I lay her down and position myself on top of her, taking in the delicious view and her scent for a moment before pressing my hips forward to enter her.

There's something different about missionary, the intimacy to it, that makes my heart beat a little faster. I can see in Felicia's eyes that she feels it too, the bond between us growing as I make love to her. I never want it to end.

I kiss her hard and long, letting myself get lost in the sweetness of her lips. None of the women I've been with have ever made me feel this way. No one has made me feel this complete or at peace with myself. I know I'm not just a celebrity to Felicia. She's with me because she wants bragging rights or to write home about how she landed a football star. She's with me ... for *me.*

I let my lips linger on hers a moment longer before pulling back, my cock twitching against her walls as I feel myself getting ready to cum.

"You can cum inside me," she says. "I want you to."

Her words are all I need to cross the finish line. I thrust my hips down onto her as hard as I can, forcing myself as deep inside her as she can take as I pump out shot after shot. Finally, I empty my load into her tight little hole, feeling the hot liquid spill out of her and onto the couch below.

Sweaty and spent, I collapse down beside her as she flips onto her side and presses her butt against my pelvis. My face nuzzles into her hair, breathing in the fruity scent of her shampoo as my heart rate begins to slow.

"Ron?"

"Yeah?" I say, wrapping my arms around her and squeezing. I want her to know she's safe here in my arms. Nothing can hurt her so long as I'm here protecting her.

"You know your Superbowl game against the Washington Commanders next week?"

"Yeah. What about it?"

"Can I ... Would you mind if I came with you? To Washington D.C. and the game."

I smile as I pull her tighter against me, my body cradling her as we spoon. "I'd like that a lot, Felicia. Of course, you can come with me and to the game."

"Good," she says, "because I think I might be falling in love with you."

"That makes two of us, babe."

7

————

FELICIA

I WAKE UP WITH HIS HAND still wrapped around my body, but loosely. It delights me to know he is that cuddly and possessive.

His one leg has gone across me and hangs on the couch's head. It is funny to see him in such an awkward, almost childish manner, so I giggle behind a palm. I don't want to be loud enough to wake him. He is sleeping so peacefully and soundly, his hard chest rising and falling gently.

The poor man must be exhausted with all the training and traveling he has to do. This is probably one of the very few nights he sleeps this long.

A smile comes across my lips as I watch his handsome face. The daylight peeping from between the spaces of the drawn blinds as they play on his face. All that dark smooth skin, his hair falling across his face, his sensual lips slightly parted in sleep. Damn, I can't think of anyone more beautiful.

I can stay here looking at him all day—so enrapturing he is to my senses—but I know we must start our day. Something tells me it is long past seven am already. As much as I would like to keep him here forever and ever, he is a star that must have his day filled. I don't have any design work today, but I should go to the grocery store for supplies and get ready for my job at the center.

Carefully, trying hard not to wake him, I gently lift his hand draped lazily across me and then slide through the space in between his legs, under the full display of his flaccid cock and balls.

I stand at the foot of the couch and look about the sitting room. It is a mess. Our clothes are strewn on the floor everywhere as if we had battled them off in a war situation.

But, having a flashback as to how desperate and needy we had both been, I realized that it had been a war...one to see who could get naked first.

Just like that, my mind goes back to all the details...Ron's tongue on my pussy, his cock filling me slowly but surely, and then him cuddling me after it was all done.

It is the latter that makes me want him again even now. The fact that he didn't turn away right after or get up and run out the door as if he was next to yesterday's trash.

It wasn't as though he was sex-starved and just needed any available pussy to sink his dick. He was still here on my couch, the scent of our lovemaking still hanging in the air, and our bodies satiated. I will be calling Stanley Steamers in the morning. We definitely took a few years off the life of my sofa.

I should get a shower first, but I fear he may wake up before I come down again and seek to rush off on an empty stomach. So, with that thought in mind, I can get breakfast ready before I go up to shower. I think it's better that way.

In the kitchen, the clock hanging on the wall proves me very wrong with my assumption of how far the morning has gone.

It is long past eight am, and the second hand is still moving along, not slowing down.

Now, I'm concerned that he has important engagements being in my house has kept him from fulfilling.

Still, I won't let him go without him eating something. Not after the two rounds of sex last night and the length of time we spent talking well into the morning.

Quickly, I get four eggs from the fridge and then bread. I wanted to make pancakes earlier, but I don't think there is time for that now.

"Fuck!" I exclaim and jump back as my rush to open the tap and fill the coffee maker makes me do it with an unnecessary zest that gets me sprayed. The cold water sends a shock to my body.

I'm only relaxed a bit when the bread—two slices each—is resting, nicely toasted, on plates, and I turn off the cooker on the omelets. I carefully lay the eggs on the plates and then proceeded to rinse mugs for the coffee.

It must be the sound of the rushing water, or maybe just my many thoughts, but I don't hear him come in. The feel of his large, muscled arms as they wrap around my stomach and pull me back against his length placing soft kisses on the side of my neck.

I jump and then laugh. "Ron!" I turn to him, mugs in one hand. "You startled me!"

He is smiling so widely, a corner of his eyes crusty with sleep. "Really? How do you think I felt when I opened my eyes and didn't see you beside me?" His morning face is so innocent and child-like. It is hard to think of it with respect to giving pleasure.

"Look," I say, pointing up to the wall clock, "It's almost nine am. You must have a ton of things to do in your celebrity life."

He shakes his head even before I finish speaking. "Nothing matters. I want to spend the entire day with you."

My heart starts pounding rapidly in my chest. "You can't be serious. Ron, you have a game next week. I imagine that you have to..."

"Rest and stare at a beautiful face for an entire day?" he cuts in. "Oh yeah."

I giggle and hit his chest playfully. "Stop! You can't be serious, Ron. You know this is not what you want to do at all."

He nods his head slowly, not blinking for a second. "You're right... What I want right now is to feed you, then feed on you, and much later feed inside of you."

I feel my panties getting wet. This dude is way out of my league
My eyes bore into his, my heart beating wildly.

8

———

RONALD

SHE IS LOOKING AT ME as though I had just offered to share part of my estate with her. Actually, with how good she fucked me last night and how much she is staring at me with those lovely eyes of hers, I just may give everything I have to her. So, captivating she is right now, standing against me, two mugs held in her hands.

Her nipples are poking into my chest, and I am sure she can feel my cock hardening.

I smell our combined scents on both of us—a mixture of sex and yesterday's cologne—and it is doing something to my senses. I don't know why I should be so fascinated by this everyday woman I just met the previous day. More confusing, still, is how relaxed and unaffected I am about the prospect.

After the number my ex-Linda did on me, I didn't think I would ever feel like this again for another woman. Instead, I want my day to revolve around this sun.

And it's not just the sex. I'm not that starved of it. There have been one or two flings. It is just something else...something lighting up my entire being in a way I cannot explain. I crave this thing so desperately...it is shocking to me.

"Let's eat," I tell her before I submit to the urge of devouring her right here on her toes. "Let me feed you, Felicia."

I see her swallow hard even as I slowly take the mugs from her, my eyes not leaving hers. I hold her hand and backpedal to the marble kitchen table. I pull out a stool for her to sit on.

I take the mugs to the coffee machine and pour us both a cup.

"Cream? Sugar?" I ask.

"Mmm," she replies and points at the cupboard just above my head.

When I set the cups on the table and take the seat adjacent to her, she still looks stunned. I wonder if I should shake her.

"Are you okay?" I ask with a little laugh.

She doesn't laugh with me. "Why are you doing this? Why are you here...with me? You are a celebrity, for goodness' sake!"

I am stung by her question, but I don't show it. I mean...just yesterday, she was admitting to something like love for me. What has changed?

"Why did you kiss me last night and let me make love to you?" I don't look at her. I placed her egg in between her toast and cut the squares diagonally.

"Don't do that," she says as I bring a piece up to her mouth.

"Do what?"

"Don't patronize me. You are famous, rich, and breathtaking. Women throw themselves at you every single day. I was just one of such. And so, what I did was not strange to you. It meant nothing. I meant nothing." Her voice has risen a note higher.

Surely, this behavior change must be something close to having a morning-after hangover from too much alcohol.

I keep the food angled at her mouth and speak very calmly. "So... What you're saying is that I sleep with all the women that come on to me?"

"Don't you?"

I feel like a scorpion has stung me. My heart stops beating for a second because of her words.

I look at her eyes, and they are just as challenging...as merciless. What the hell have I done or said to make her so touchy this morning?

I drop the bread onto the plate again and wait for her to say something...something else that will reverse this thing that she has dropped on us in the middle of a lovely breakfast she has prepared. Surely, it must all be some mistake. She will realize it, and she will make redress.

But nothing else comes out of her mouth. She just stays staring at me.

"Come," I tell her finally, getting up from the stool.

She looks confused, so I hold her hand and pull her up.

"What's going on, Ron? Where are we going?"

I don't know the layout of her house, but I guess the door that is her room and realizes that I am right.

I like how simple and neat the space is. It makes it appear much bigger than it is and gives it a homely feeling. I can imagine her falling into the well-made bed at the end of a stressful day. I wonder if she touches herself on horny nights. Heck, I wonder if any other guy has ever touched her on this bed.

Thinking in that direction fills me with acute discomfort, and I can't explain why.

I quickly lead her to the bathroom and put on the shower to "warm."

She frees herself of my hold. "What are you doing, Ron?" She folds her arms across her breasts. I resist the urge to try to get her hands down so I can keep looking at those beauties.

"We have to take a bath, Felicia. Please, get in."

She looks at me for a few seconds but doesn't enter the shower casing. I go in with her and close us in.

The water is cascading from her hair to the rest of her body; I see how calm it makes her. Her eyes are closed, and she raises her face to the spray.

"Feels good, right?" I say, watching her.

"Hmm," she agrees. She is so relaxed that she has forgotten to keep fighting.

"That's how you make me feel too, Felicia."

Her eyes fly open, but I am already hugging her from behind, pressing her against the tiled walls. My hardening cock is lodged against her butt. It grows fuller with every movement she makes.

"What are you doing?" she hisses in a voice that is supposed to sound cold but ends up betraying her with how breathless it sounds.

"Bathing you," I say and grab a bar of soap from the holder. I release her from the wall and begin running the soap over her breasts. I do it carefully and intentionally, focusing on her nipples. When my hands reach down to her stomach, she is totally relaxed against me; my erection wedged between her ass cheeks. Her neck is arched, and my mouth is close to her ear. I lap at the inside with my tongue softly.

"No, Felicia," I whisper in my sexiest voice, "I don't do this with all the ladies that throw themselves at me. And, for the record, I don't think that's what you did yesterday." I end my speech by licking her ear.

She shivers and whimpers slightly.

She is moving against me now, wriggling her legs and butt in an almost frantic manner. I know what that means—she wants me... And I haven't even done anything yet.

"I will not make love to you again until you understand that you are special to me, Felicia. I know we just met yesterday, but I understand a spark when it happens. I feel something for you just as I know, somewhere in your heart, you do for me too. Sometimes things happen, and people are brought together for a reason."

I rinse the soap off my right hand and take my fingers to her crotch.

I am not even touching her clit yet when she shivers and bucks against me. It is good that I am standing firmly; her need will have thrown me off balance.

"Fuck me, Ron," she moans. "Please."

I shake my head though she can't see. "You have to understand, Felicia."

$$9$$

FELICIA

IT IS TORTURE IN EVERY WAY, sitting across him like this in a restaurant. Since its mid-morning, there are no candle lights and soft romantic music, but everything about the man seated opposite me is getting into my head.

Of course, it's not helping that he has that stupid smirk on his lips and the amusement in his eyes.

Damn!

He knows what he's doing to me. He knows what's happening to me.

Beneath the finely designed table, my legs are jumping fast. A nervous habit I can't help. They won't stay still. My body is tense and on high alert, waiting for what will happen next. Even the other diners' background talk all around us seems too loud though it is all nothing but an incoherent buzz.

I can also feel my skin crawling with goosebumps, knowing my cheeks are red.

But all the discomfort is nothing compared to how badly my clit is hurting. Swollen and wet, it craves attention. It craves a not so gentle hand rubbing until the tension is released.

Yet, I am seated here waiting for the smiling waitress to bring our order. Even her smile looks too much. I don't have an appetite for her food. I don't think I will have any such desire until I have been appeased.

"Relax," Ron says to me with that smile still on his face.

I want to be angry with him, but I can't be... Not when he is looking at me with those sexy eyes that make me want to jump him right here.

"How did we end up here?"

He shrugs and grins. "You know, we spent too long taking a bath in the bathroom. Then, we came out again to cold coffee, eggs, and toasts. It was a disaster. We had to leave the house to find food...and to give ourselves a little air to breathe..." He winks at me.

"You know what I mean."

For a second, I am lost in the beauty of his face, though he is wearing one of my baseball caps very low on his head.

For some reason, he thinks it is enough to disguise to save him from being recognized and accosted for pictures.

The price of fame!

"Are you here?" He touches my hand on the table. I jerk it away from reflex and blink myself back to the moment.

"You worked me up good in that shower, Ron, with all that soaping and rubbing." There is no need to feel shy about how frustrated I feel. I must let him know. "You worked me up and then left me hangin'? I will never forgive you for that."

He leans closer. "I worked both of us up." He drops his voice a bit and replies, "Why do you believe that I don't feel all that you feel? You have the mindset that this is all a game to me, right? You still don't understand what you are doing to me?"

At that, I was at a loss for words. I won't lie to myself; In the end, I still won't get the man. Why is he pretending like we both don't know how this will end? Yes, the previous night, I was caught in the sweet euphoria of it all and said things he went along with, but isn't it long enough for him to stop the act?

I am not about to say another thing. When the waitress brings our order on a large tray, she spreads it out onto the table.

Ron doesn't allow both of them to make eye contact.

When she and her smile get lost, I pick up my fork and blurt out, "I want you, Ron."

He nods at his plate as if I am talking about a weather forecast, he heard about already. "Let's hope you learn before the day ends then."

He adds sunglasses to his supposed "disguise" at the first store in the mall we enter.

He has brought me here to spend his money on anything, he had said to me.

Nonetheless, the boy in the next store we enter recognizes him and calls unto his other colleagues, who gasp and look like they are about to faint.

Like some forgotten rag, I stand by the corner and watch the scene before me.

Ron seems to be born to do this. His smiles and words of cheer feel deep and real. Those kids will spend the next couple of nights thinking about them. Little will they know the star likes to hide, only to be found by people like them. Little will they know he wants a quiet life and is practicing with a girl that already has that.

Of course, I can't tell him that last part when he returns to me, the forgotten, and hurries us out of the shop before others start coming.

"What a ruckus you cause when you are recognized." I tease as we head back to the car. Shopping with Ron when so many people are around has proven to be a bad idea. *Thank goodness for E-commerce!*

"Imagine how Washington will be when we go for the game."

I look up at him as we wait for a car to pass before crossing the road. "You really will take me with you?"

His expression is one of keen disappointment and hurt. I almost want to apologize.

He shakes his head at me mournfully. "It's afternoon, and you still have these negative things in your head. What else can I do? Is it because we couldn't shop? Here... I will give you, my card. Is that okay?" He stretches a card to me.

I don't know what to say to make him stop looking at me in that disappointing manner, and so I just keep looking at him, trying to settle my unbelieving heart.

"There's one more place you have to be, isn't it?" he asks, looking tired.

10

———

RONALD

I FOLLOW HER TO THE COMMUNITY CENTER. Her boss, Darcie, is shocked and delighted to see me.

She gives me a big hug like a long-lost relative. "Ronald! What a pleasant surprise! What are you doing here?"

What can I even tell her? I don't think Felicia will be particularly delighted to have her coordinator know she fucked their guest speaker in a matter of hours.

The second's tick by as I think of something appropriate to say.

"Well," Felicia says from beside me, "he reached out to me and asked if he could come back here and see the kids again... You know...like, help out with whatever is happening today."

Whether Darcie is suspicious or not, her gasp of excitement sounds very real. She hugs me again. "The youths will be so honored. It's a privilege they don't get have all that often. I can imagine how pumped they will be." She does a little hopping on her feet and then strolls away, sure to spread the news of my presence to the other volunteers.

Felicia and I didn't say anything after her coordinator left.

Finally, I move to begin unfolding seats. "You lie very convincingly." I make it sound like a compliment.

"It was technically the truth," she says in a voice that dares me to contest her.

She begins unfolding chairs too, and my eyes stray to her.

She's dressed in a crop top and a black skirt that stops just above the knee. Her long legs end in a pair of white sneakers that accentuate her ankles in a sexy way. I want to kiss those ankles and then work my way upwards to her lap, her inner thighs, and then...

"Delighted about your upcoming game?" She inquires, cutting into the hot sexual image of her I am having in my head.

Her tone is more relaxed, and now it makes me suspicious. I chance a glance at her, but her head is bent, hard at work.

Why does she sound so sweet? Can it be that she's horny and desperate enough to try and get me to have sex with her? This is new.

"I am delighted about every game."

"I thought you didn't like the perks of your job?"

I knew she was teasing. I level a glare at her even though I know she's not looking at me.

"Not funny!"

She looks up at me and smiles in a naughty way. "Not laughing either."

Now, I know she's trying to use her goodwill to bait me. But it won't happen. I had fallen for that before, and it didn't end well. Felicia's sudden antics result from sexual frustration, and she means no harm; I have groomed myself not to fall for whiles anymore.

"What are you playing at, Felicia?" I stand, arms folded in front of me, waiting for her answer.

"How excited are you about what you will be playing in Washington next week?" She places her hands on akimbo too and looks at me. "That was the question, Mr."

I see how she puts her chest out, her breasts pointing at me enticingly. Her eyes glazed over with arousal.

Even in this public place, my dick can decide to react to the raw need in her eyes. It is too visible to be avoided. Her entire being is calling out to me. If I stare a second more, I may lose it, demand for trust or not.

I turn away quickly and find something else to keep myself busy.

"The Washington Commanders are a solid team, but I'm hoping

we can beat them in their territory. What a wonderful way to win the Superbowl Game. What do you think?"

"Yeah," she says, but there's no spirit in her words.

Later that night, we lay in bed cuddling; she stuns me with a question.

"What happened with you and your ex-girlfriend?"

My heart does a flip-flop.

I don't talk about her ever. Things are better left unsaid. So, trust me when I say she is not worth the energy to explain.

But she wiggles her butt against me when I don't answer. "Ron?"

"Ahhhh..." I wonder how much I can say before it all turns dangerous. I want to leave the past in the past.

"If you don't want to tell a total stranger your business, I understand. It's fine. I..."

I kiss her shoulder blade. "Stop! You are not a stranger. Don't go there."

"Ron, I appreciate that you are still here this long, but you don't have to pretend. We both know this is just a pleasant fling or a 'booty call' for both of us if you want to be crude. After this, we may..."

"We may what?" Suddenly, I cross over her, so we are lying facing each other. I am shocked to see moisture in her eyes. "What's wrong, Felicia?" I feel my heart breaking into pieces.

"It's just that... I want this to last, but then it all seems too good to be true. I want this not just for one day." She puts a palm to my cheek.

"Are you are saying that good things don't last?"

"Wasn't it good with your last girlfriend? Was she also not a rich celebrity...like me? And things just had to end, right? A celebrity couldn't keep up with the demeaning demands of dating an average nobody and..."

"Linda was a supermodel!" I burst out in a voice that makes her search my eyes. I shouldn't raise my voice, but I can't take her misconceptions anymore. Her distrust makes my soul ache. "She was famous enough to be selfish and arrogant. She did everything to me and knew she could get away with it."

"Get away with what?" The way she is looking at me makes me know I can't help but spill all.

"Linda cheated on me, Felicia. Not once...not twice. She knew how much I loved her, and so she rubbed it in my face. It took a lot to make the decision to leave her. She thought I wouldn't be able to. I thought I wouldn't either but drowning in alcohol was doing me no good. I was missing practices...games.... Fuck!" It is like I have been thrown into a dark hole again.

But Felicia moves closer and hugs me. She finds me in that place that I am. "If I ever have what Linda had," she says to me, drawing back, "I won't toy with it like that. Heck, I will value it for all time."

I take some time to deliberate over her words. I want to be sure she is saying what I think she is saying. "Felicia," I say calmly, "you can have me... You have me. That is the point I have wanted you to see all day."

Her eyes look so mournful. It feels like she is burying the dead. "I...I... like to be realistic, Ron. That's all. I don't build sandcastles in the air with my thoughts."

A spear to my heart, I grab her hand. "Am I not real enough? I am here. Flesh and blood. This can all be a start of something wonderful."

She shakes her head slightly. "You are a fantasy, Ron... An enigma... Something the hot girls can afford to point to and say 'uh... I want that one.' But, for girls like me, you remain an image we masturbate to at night."

I look at her for a long time before carefully selecting my words. "If the real thing is here, what do you need an image for? Hell, why won't you open your eyes and see...and feel?"

"What is there to feel?"

I am by her legs in another sudden motion, turning her to lay straight.

"What are you doing?" she asks me.

She knows what I am doing.

She cooperates as I pull her legs apart and then take down her nightie shorts.

"Raise your knees for me, Felicia. I want to taste you," I say, my mouth already against her pussy.

She does it without arguments.

I look into her eyes for a moment, see the desire there, and then I answer it.

She cries out and tries to pull away when I put my mouth to her clit.

My arms are around her waist, holding her pelvis down to my mouth so she can't escape.

I tongue her wet opening and then move up to the clit again, licking and sucking it with zest.

"Fuuuck..." she moans.

I give little moans of my own, too, as I suck, my hands going upwards to tease her nipples.

"Ron... Ohhh..."

"You like this?" I say against her pussy.

I raise my head slightly to see her nodding frantically.

"Please..." She starts to whimper. "Ron, please..."

I rub her clit very fast with my fingers and look up at her. Her eyes are closed, and she's turning her head from side to side. "What do you want, Felicia? You have to tell me. What do you see? What do you feel? Talk to me. I need to hear the words I will not ask again?"

"You," she repeatedly answers, over and over. I give a small chuckle and replace my fingers with my tongue again.

My dick is trying to burst out of my shorts by this time. I want to be in her so badly. I want to ride her hard until she starts babbling in another tongue, but I must put myself under control. How I feel about her, fucking her will make this about me, and I don't want it to be. This was all about her and how much I wanted to please her and be her every fantasy.

"Don't hold back," I tell her when the mounting pleasure makes her start to squirm and retreat. She's trying to clamp her legs together, but I raise her butt, bringing her closer to my mouth. "You can cum for me, honey."

"Ron, I..." She is breathless, panting heavily.

"I am here, baby. I will always be here."

I know she wants to cum, but she is holding back for some reason. It seems like something in her mind is fighting it. It's almost like she can't trust me with her cum.

I put two fingers in her pussy and fuck her that way.

"Open your eyes and look at me, Felicia." I see how much of a struggle she is putting up. "Look at me, baby. Hey..."

She opens her eyes and props herself up on her elbows and meets my eyes. There is a resolve in hers. I know she wants to make a demand I can't refuse.

I know I will do it. Whatever it is.

"Please, fuck me, Ron." I am taken aback for a moment. "Just fuck me, please. I am tired of this back and forth all day. It's driving me crazy."

My cock twitches wildly in my shorts. There is only so much I can take. The arousal in her eyes is enough to break every control and restraint inside me.

"Please, Ron..." She falls back unto the bed as if resigned to the fate of never getting satisfaction from me. That breaks me further. I don't want her to suffer for lack of the soul-reaching bliss that only I can give her.

I take my fingers out of her and pull down my shorts. Mr. hard dick is delighted.

"You drive me crazy, babe," I admit just, so we are clear that the desire is mutual. "I have wanted to make love to you all morning. I just needed us to be on the same page."

She props herself up again. "We are, Ron. I promise you."

I almost laugh at how desperately she speaks and looks at me.

I put my cock to the pussy lips and tease her with it, rubbing her moisture up and down.

"Do you trust me?" I ask her.

"Yes. Yes..." She moves her legs, impatiently wanting me to fill her up. "You are here, and you are real."

"Yeah?" I beat my cock on her clit for some seconds.

"Yeah. You say you want me too, right?"

I nod enthusiastically. "Not just sexually, babe. I want you to be there when I win the game. I want everyone to see you...see me with you... Isn't that trustworthy enough?"

She pauses her desperation and just looks at me. "Don't play with my emotions, Ron."

I push my cock into her slowly, watching her eyes. "Do I look like I'm playing?"

She rolls her eyes back and shakes her head.

She is so wet and delicious. There's no need to waste any time.

Her moan fills my ears as I pick up the pace.

"Yes, Ron... Right there," she pants as I go even faster. "Don't stop. Don't. Uhhh..."

I don't have any intention to. This is too good—all of this...all of her. I know that I want it forever after today.

"I'm about to cum, Ron," she says soon enough.

"Me too," I confess with a groan.

While I thrust, I rub her clit with a thumb.

"Oh... Oh..."

She stills suddenly, clenching her stomach, and then she relaxes, twitching almost violently just as I hit her with the last stroke too.

"Fuuuck!" I empty myself into her.

We stay joined like that, breathing heavily.

I know with all certainty that she is mine. I want to be together forever with her for as long as she will have me. My bet is for the rest of our lives.

Felicia finally catches her breath "I can't wait for you to meet my mother and sisters. They are force to be reckoned with and are going to love you. The last I heard; your friend Lee was going hot and heavy with my sister Sharon. I'll talk with Pamela in the morning to see about getting the gang together. So, get ready my love. You're about to experience a sisterhood like none other. Our motto is "We don't die; we multiply!!!" lol.

"Now, wake that boy up. You are far from finished."

ABOUT THE AUTHOR

Olivia Houde is your hottest new author of sweet romance! She's an advocate for instalove, spicy scenes, endearing characters, and happily ever afters. Her stories are chock full of true love and happy endings and are sure to make any reader's heart swell.

www.oliviahoude.com

Check out my other books now on amazon.com:

Saving Grace:
https://www.amazon.com/dp/B09QP3K7X2
Deep Impact:
https://www.amazon.com/dp/B09P6HH8DV
Take Your Time:
https://www.amazon.com/dp/B09KPXWFYZ
Make Me Yours:
https://www.amazon.com/dp/B09K5TCQSZ
Love After Pain:
https://www.amazon.com/dp/B09JLNLPY1

THANKS FOR READING!